SELECTED
FROM

The Lost Angel

♥ ♡

MARY HIGGINS CLARK

WRITERS' VOICES

SIGNAL HILL™

P U B L I C A T I O N S

ATTENTION READERS: We would like to hear what you think about our books. Please send your comments or suggestions to:

Signal Hill Publications
P.O. Box 131
Syracuse, NY 13210-0131

•   •   •

SIGNAL HILL™

PUBLICATIONS

Additional material
© 1990 Signal Hill Publications
A publishing imprint of Laubach Literacy International

10 9 8 7 6 5 4 3 2

First printing: April 1990

ISBN 0-929631-13-7

Cover design by Paul Davis Studio
Interior design by Barbara Huntley

Acknowledgments

We gratefully acknowledge the generous support of the following foundations and corporations that made the publication of WRITERS' VOICES and NEW WRITERS' VOICES possible: The Vincent Astor Foundation; Booth Ferris Foundation; Exxon Corporation; James Money Management, Inc.; Scripps Howard Foundation; Uris Brothers Foundation, Inc.; The H.W. Wilson Foundation; and Weil, Gotshal & Manges Foundation Inc.

This book could not have been realized without the kind and generous cooperation of the author, Mary Higgins Clark, her agent McIntosh and Otis, Inc., and her publisher Simon and Schuster, Inc. We are particularly grateful to Mrs. Clark for writing a special note to the reader of this book.

Our thanks to Paul Davis Studio and Myrna Davis, Paul Davis, and Jeanine Esposito for their inspired design of WRITERS' VOICES. Thanks also to Barbara Huntley for her sensitive attention to the interior design of this series.

CONTENTS

ABOUT WRITERS' VOICES

"I want to read what others do—what I see people reading in libraries, on the subway, and at home."
                    Mamie Moore, a literacy student,
                                Brooklyn, New York

Writers' Voices is our response to Mamie Moore's wish:

- the wish to step forward into the reading community,
- the wish to have access to new information,
- the wish to read to her grandchildren,
- the wish to read for the joy of reading.

NOTE TO THE READER

"What we are familiar with, we cease to see. The writer shakes up the familiar scene, and, as if by magic, we see a new meaning in it."
Anaïs Nin

Writers' Voices invites you to discover new meaning. One way to discover new meaning is to learn something new. Another is to see in a new way something you already know.

Writers' Voices is a series of books. Each book contains selections from one or more writers' work. We chose the selections because the writers' voices can be clearly heard. Also, they deal with experiences that are interesting to think about and discuss.

If you are a new reader, you may want to have a selection read aloud to you, perhaps more than once. This will free you to enjoy the piece, to hear the language used, and to think about its meaning. Even if you are a more experienced reader, you may enjoy hearing the

7

selection read aloud before reading it silently to yourself.

Each selection is set in a framework to expand your understanding of the selection. The framework includes a chapter that tells about the writer's life.

You may also find chapters about the characters, the plot, and when or where the story took place. These will help you begin thinking about the selection. They will also help you understand what may be unfamiliar to you.

We encourage you to read *actively*. An active reader does many things—while reading, and before and after reading—that help him or her better understand and enjoy a book. Here are some suggestions of things you can do:

Before Reading

• Read the front and back covers of the book, and look at the cover illustration. Ask yourself what you expect the book to be about, based on this information.

• Think about why you want to read this book. What do you want to discover, and what questions will be answered?

• Look at the contents page. Decide which chapters you want to read and in what order you want to read them.

During Reading

• Try to stay with the rhythm of the language. If you find any words or sentences you don't understand, keep reading to see if the meaning becomes clear. If it doesn't, go back and reread the difficult part or discuss it with others.

• Try to put yourself into the story.

• Ask yourself questions as you read. For example: Do I believe this story or this chapter? Why?

After Reading

• Ask yourself if the story makes you see any of your own experiences in a new way.

• Ask yourself if the story has given you any new information.

• Keep a journal in which you can write down your thoughts about what you have read, and save new words you have learned.

• Look over the questions at the end of the book. They are meant to help you discover more about what you have read and how it relates to you—as a person, as a reader, as a writer. Try those questions that seem most interesting to you.

• Talk about what you have read with other readers.

Good writing should make you think after you put the book down. Whether you are a beginning reader, a more experienced reader, or a teacher of reading, we encourage you to take time to think about these books and to discuss your thoughts with others. If you want to read more books by the author of the selections, you can go to your bookstore or library to find them.

When you are finished with the book, we hope you will write to our editors about your reactions. We want to know your thoughts about our books, and what they have meant to you.

SPECIAL NOTE
TO THE READER FROM
MARY HIGGINS CLARK

I get up very early in the morning and write. Sometimes I will write straight through the day; at other times, I write for only a few hours, depending on my schedule. I feel guilty if I'm not writing. It is so much a part of my nature. Even when I'm not writing on my computer, I'm writing in my head.

The key word in writing suspense stories is "suppose." I begin with something I know about and then ask myself, "Suppose this or that happened."

When I start a book, I go through my mind and take pieces of things I have read about or experienced. I also keep a diary, as I have since I was very young. My diaries are a wonderful help to my novels. I can read them and know what I was like at all different ages.

I write about ordinary people whose lives have been invaded by danger. People can imagine themselves in the shoes of my characters. We all hang by a thread, and there are many things we cannot choose about our lives. It's how we react to the good and bad things that happen to us that counts. My characters are strong. When trouble strikes, they react well. They carry on.

My main character is always a woman. She is strong but vulnerable. She leads a normal life, until suddenly something terrible happens to her.

My stories take place over a short period of time—sometimes a weekend, sometimes a week. The fast pace of the story makes for more excitement.

I always plan for an emotional ending. At the end of a suspense story, the problem is solved. The bad guy has been punished. And the heroine has achieved satisfaction.

I started making up scary stories when I was a child. And I loved to read mysteries and suspense novels. So when I started writing, I decided to try suspense. I have been lucky to be successful at it. But even if I weren't, I would keep on writing. I'm doing what I like to do.

ABOUT THE SELECTION FROM
THE LOST ANGEL

Mary Higgins Clark wrote *The Lost Angel* in 1986. It is the story of Susan Ahearn's search for her kidnapped daughter, Jamie. The story goes back and forth between what is happening to Susan and what is happening to Jamie.

Susan and her husband, Jeff, are separated. Susan has custody of Jamie. Jeff kidnapped Jamie from her nursery school and disappeared with her. The first part of the story takes place in Chicago, where Susan lives.

The second part of the story takes place in Manhattan, in New York City. It is the day before Christmas.

You may want to look at the map of midtown Manhattan on page 38. The map shows the places that are referred to in the story.

Like most towns and cities, New York City is very beautiful at Christmastime. A giant tree with decorations is put up next to the skating rink in Rockefeller Center. The ceremony of lighting this tree is shown on television every year.

Department stores have window displays created especially for the Christmas season. One of the most beautiful is presented by the Lord and Taylor department store. The Lord and Taylor windows show old-fashioned Christmas scenes, with dolls that move and turn as they celebrate the season.

All year round, but especially at Christmastime, people like to take horse-drawn carriage rides in Central Park. The carriage drivers line up on Central Park South, waiting for customers.

The Port Authority Bus Terminal is one of the world's largest bus stations. Thousands of people go through the terminal every day, to catch commuter and long-distance buses.

Perhaps this story will make you think about a time when someone you knew was lost. Perhaps it will remind you of a time when you had family problems during a holiday period.

SELECTED FROM
The Lost Angel
♥ ♡
MARY HIGGINS CLARK

IT SNOWED THE night before Christmas Eve. By dawn the storm began to let up and uncertain sun broke through the clouds.

At six o'clock, Susan Ahearn got out of bed, turned up the thermostat and made coffee. Shivering, she closed her hands over the cup. She always felt so cold; it was probably all the weight she had lost since Jamie disappeared.

One hundred and ten pounds wasn't enough to cover her five feet eight inches; her eyes the same blue-green as Jamie's seemed too big for her face; her cheekbones had become prominent; even her chestnut hair had darkened to a deep brown that accentuated the pale, drawn look that was now habitual.

She felt infinitely older than twenty-eight; three months ago that important birthday had been spent following one more blind lead. The child discovered in a Wisconsin foster home had not been Jamie. She hurried back under the covers while warm air whistled and grumbled through the isolated house twenty-two miles west of Chicago.

It had been a long night. Most of it she had spent awake, trying to overcome the fear that was her constant companion. Suppose she never found Jamie? Suppose Jamie became one of those children who had simply disappeared? Now to stave off the emptiness of the house, Susan began to pretend.

She envisioned Jamie in her red and white flannel nightgown padding across the room and climbing into bed with her. "Your feet are freezing. . . ."

Her arms around Jamie. Tucking the blankets around her. "Now about New York on Christmas Eve. After our ride through Central Park in the horse and carriage, we'll have lunch at the Plaza. That's a big, beautiful hotel. And right across the street . . ."

"We'll look in the toy store . . ."

"The most famous toy store in the world. It's called F A O Schwarz. It has trains and dolls and puppets and books and everything."

"I can pick out three presents . . ."

"I thought it was two. Okay, we'll make it three."

"And then we'll visit the baby Jesus in St. Pat's. . . ."

"It's really St. Patrick's Cathedral, but we Irish are a friendly group. Everyone calls it St. Pat's. . . ."

"Tell me about the tree . . . and the windows like fairyland . . ."

Susan gulped the last of the coffee over the lump in her throat. The phone began to ring and she tried to quell the wild leap of hope as she reached for it. Jamie! Let it be Jamie!

It was her mother calling from Florida. The heartsick tone that had become her mother's normal speaking voice since Jamie's disappearance was especially marked today. Determinedly, Susan forced her voice to sound positive. "No,

Mother. No word. Of course I would have phoned you. . . . It's difficult for all of us. No, I'm sure I want to stay here. Don't forget she did phone once . . . For God's sake, Mother, no, I don't think she's dead. Give me a break. Jeff is her father. In his way he loves her. . . ."

She hung up in tears, biting her lip to keep from dissolving into angry hysterics. Even her mother did not know how bad it really was.

So far, six indictments had been issued for Jeff's arrest. The entrepreneur she thought she'd married was really an international jewel thief. The reason for this remote house in this remote suburb was because it had made a good hiding place for him. She'd learned the truth last spring when FBI agents had come to arrest Jeff just after he had left on one of his "business trips." He never returned, so she'd put the house up for sale. She was making arrangements to move to New York—the four years she'd spent in college there had been the happiest of her life. Then a few weeks after his disappearance Jeff went to Jamie's nursery school and took her away. That was seven months ago.

On the drive to work Susan could not rid herself of the fear her mother's call had triggered. *Do you think Jamie is dead?* Jeff was absolutely irresponsible. When Jamie was six months old, he'd left her alone in the house to go out for cigarettes. When she was two years old, he didn't notice that she'd waded out in water over her head. A lifeguard had saved her. How could he possibly be taking care of her now? Why had he *wanted* her?

The real-estate office was festive with Christmas decorations. They were a nice group, the sixteen people she worked with, and Susan appreciated the hopeful glances they offered her each morning. All of them wanted to hear good news about Jamie. Today, nobody was interested in doing much work, but she kept busy by reviewing papers for future closings.

Joan Rogers, the agent at the next desk, was reading a magazine. With a stab of pain Susan saw the title of the article: "Children Aren't Always Angels on Christmas Day." Whimsical photographs of children in white robes and halos dotted the page.

Susan stared, then reached over and frantically grabbed the magazine from Joan's hand. The angel in the upper right-hand corner. A little girl. Hair so blond it was almost white. But the eyes. The mouth. The rounded curve of the cheek. "Oh God," Susan whispered. She pulled open her desk drawer, fumbled through its contents and found a Magic Marker. With trembling fingers she covered the bright hair of the child in the photograph with the warm brown tone of the pen and watched as the angel's image became identical with the framed picture on her desk.

Jamie looked thoughtfully out the window of the bedroom at the cold winter scene outside and tried not to listen to the quarreling voices. Daddy and Tina were mad at each other again. Someone in the apartment building had shown Daddy her picture in the magazine. Daddy was yelling, "What are you trying to pull? We'll all land in jail. How many other times did she pose?"

They'd come to New York at the end of the summer, and Daddy started to take a lot of trips without them. Tina said she was bored and might as well do a little modeling. But the woman she went to said, "I don't need any more of your type, but I can use the little girl."

Posing for the picture of the angel was easy. They'd asked her to think about something nice, so she'd thought about Christmas Eve and how Mommy and she had planned to spend it in New York this year. Now she was in New York and she was near every place she and Mommy had planned to go—but it wasn't the same at all with Daddy and Tina.

"I asked you how many times she posed!" Daddy yelled.

"Twice, three times," Tina shouted.

That was a fib. She had gone to the studio lots of times when Daddy was away.

Now Tina was saying, "What do you expect me to do while you're gone? Read Dr. Seuss and play jacks?"

On the street below people were hurrying as though they were cold. It had snowed during the night, but this snow melted under the wheels of the cars and turned into dirty piles of slush. It was only from the corner of her eye that she could see Central Park where the snow was as pretty as it was supposed to be.

Jamie swallowed over the lump in her throat. She knew that the baby Jesus came on the night of Christmas Eve. Every single day she had prayed that this year when God brought the baby Jesus, he would bring Mommy too. But Daddy told her that Mommy was still very sick. And tonight they were going to get on a plane again and fly to someplace else. It sounded like bananas. No. It was ba-ha-mas.

"Jamie!"

Tina's voice was so angry when she called her. She knew Tina didn't like her. She was always telling Daddy, "She's your kid."

Daddy was sitting at the table, reading the newspaper. Daddy wasn't ever mean to her. The only time he'd slapped her was when she tried to phone Mommy. She'd just heard Mommy's voice on the phone saying "Please leave a message" when Daddy caught her. She managed to say, "I hope you're getting better, Mommy, I miss you," before Daddy slammed down the phone and slapped her. After that he locked the phone whenever he and Tina weren't right there. Daddy said that Mommy was so sick, she would hurt herself trying to talk. But Mommy didn't sound sick when she said, "Please leave a message."

Daddy was frowning and he sounded mad when he read out loud, "The servants think the shorter of the two thieves may have been a woman." Then Daddy said, "I told you that outfit was a giveaway."

Tina leaned over his shoulder while she read: *"May be an inside job.* What more do you want?"

"Just as well we're leaving," Daddy said. "We've overworked this town."

Jamie thought of all the apartments they had gone to see. "Do we have to go to ba-ha-mas?" she asked. It sounded so far away. Farther and farther away from Mommy. "I liked the apartment yesterday," she urged. She toyed with the cornflakes, turning the spoon around in them. "Remember you told that lady that you thought it was just what you were looking for?"

Tina laughed. "Well, in a way it was, kiddo."

Jamie remembered how yesterday the woman who showed them the apartment had said what a beautiful family they were. Daddy and Tina were all dressed up in the clothes they wore when they looked at apartments, and Tina's hair was pulled back in a bun and she didn't have much makeup on.

After breakfast Tina and Daddy went into their bedroom. Jamie decided to put on the purple pants and striped long-sleeved shirt she'd been wearing the day Daddy had come to school to say Mommy was sick and he had to take her right home.

She brushed her hair and was always surprised to see how funny it looked now. It was exactly the color of Tina's hair.

When she went back into the living room, Daddy and Tina were dressed to go out. Daddy was carrying a briefcase that looked heavy. "I won't be sorry to leave this place tonight," he was saying. Jamie didn't like it here either. She knew it was nice to live only a block from Central Park, but this apartment was dark and messy and the furniture was old and the rug had a tear in it.

"Tina and I are going out for a while," Daddy told her. "I'll double-lock the door so you'll be safe. You read or watch television."

Jamie managed to smile back at him as her eyes flickered over to the telephone. *Daddy had forgotten to put the lock on it. When they left she was going to call Mommy again. She wanted to talk to Mommy about Christmas. Daddy wouldn't know.*

She waited a few minutes to be sure they were gone. Then she picked up the receiver. She had made herself say the number every single night before she went to sleep so she wouldn't forget it.

The key turned in the door. She heard Daddy curse and she dropped the phone even before he grabbed it from her. He listened, heard the dial tone, then put the receiver down and snapped the lock around it before he said, "If it weren't Christmas Eve, I'd smack you one."

He was gone again. Jamie hunched in the big chair, wrapped her arms around her legs and laid her head on her knees. She knew she was too big to cry. She was almost four and a half. Even so, she had to bite her lip to keep it from trembling. But after a minute she was able to play the pretend game.

Mommy was with her and they were going to have their special Christmas Eve. First they would go for a ride through Central Park. Then they would have lunch at the big hotel. After lunch, they'd go right across the street into the toy store F A O Swarzzz. . . . She'd pick out two toys. No, Jamie thought, Mommy said I could pick out three toys. "We'll walk down Fifth Avenue to visit the baby Jesus and then . . ."

Tina said she was such a pest always asking where everything was. But now she knew exactly how to go to Fifth Avenue from here and how to find all the places she and Mommy planned to see together.

The phone number of the magazine was on the masthead. The operator who finally answered tried to be helpful. "I'm sorry, but there's just about nobody here. A child model? That information would be in accounting and that's

closed. Can you call on the twenty-
sixth?''

In a torrent of words Susan told her
about Jamie. ''You've absolutely got to
help me. How do you pay a child who
poses? Don't you have an address?''

The operator cut in. ''Hold on. There's
got to be a way to find out.''

When the operator came back on, she
was triumphant. ''I reached one of the
editors at home. The children we used
for that article were from the Lehman
Model Agency. Here's the number.''

Susan was put through to Dora Lehman. Lehman's strident but friendly voice
said, ''Sure, Jamie's one of my kids. Sure,
she's around. She did a job last week.''

Dora Lehman did not have an address
for Jamie. ''That Tina character used to
pick up Jamie's checks here. But I do
have a phone number.''

Susan scribbled the number, wild with
impatience.

Joan stopped her from dialing. ''You'll
only tip them off. We've got to get the

New York police. They can trace the address. You get yourself booked on a plane."

Someone looked up the flight schedules. The next plane she could catch was leaving O'Hare at noon. But when she tried to make a reservation the clerk almost laughed. "There isn't an empty seat on a plane leaving Chicago today," she said. Pleading finally got her to a vice-president. "You get out here," he told her. "We'll get you on that flight even if we have to bump the pilot."

Joan finished talking to the police in New York just as Susan hung up the phone. It took Susan a moment to realize that Joan's face was somber. "Jeff was just arrested for a robbery he and that woman—Tina—he's living with committed last night. A neighbor thinks she saw Jamie and the woman come by in a cab as he was being put in a squad car. If Tina knows that Jeff is in custody, God knows where she'll disappear with Jamie."

* * *

Daddy and Tina weren't gone long. Both hands were on eleven when they got back. Tina said to put her coat on because they were going to Bloomingdale's.

It wasn't fun to shop with Tina. Jamie could tell that even the lady who sold them the clothes was surprised that Tina didn't act as though she cared what she bought. She said, "Oh, she needs a couple of bathing suits, and some shorts and shirts. That should do for her."

Then they went to the toy department. "Your father said you can pick out a couple of things," Tina told her.

She didn't really want anything. The dolls with their shiny button eyes and frilly dresses didn't look nearly as nice as the Minnie Mouse rag doll she always used to sleep with at home. But Tina looked so mad when she said she didn't want anything that she pointed to some books and asked for them.

They took a cab back to the apartment, but when the driver pulled up to the curb, Tina started to act funny. There were two police cars parked there and Jamie saw Daddy walking between two policemen. She started to point to him, but Tina pinched Jamie's knee and said to the driver, "I forgot something. Take us back to Bloomingdale's, please."

Jamie shrunk back on the seat. Daddy had talked about the police this morning. Was Daddy in trouble? She didn't dare ask Tina.

Back in Bloomingdale's, Tina shopped only for herself. She bought a suitcase, a dress, a coat and hat and big dark glasses. When Tina paid for everything, she cut off all the tags and told the saleswoman she'd decided to wear her new clothes right away.

When they left Bloomingdale's she looked like a different person.

Jamie was so hungry. All day she'd had only cornflakes and orange juice.

Near the corner she saw a hot dog and soda cart with an umbrella over it. Timidly Jamie tugged at Tina's sleeve.

"Could I have ... Is it all right if I have ..." For some reason there was a big knot in her throat. She was so hungry. She didn't know why Daddy was with the policemen and she knew Tina didn't like her.

Tina had been trying to signal a cab. "Oh, for God's sake," she said. "All right. Make it snappy."

Jamie asked for a hot dog with mustard and a Coke. The cab came up before the man added mustard, and Tina said, "Hurry up! Skip the mustard."

In the cab, Jamie tried to eat carefully so there wouldn't be any crumbs. The driver turned and said to Tina, "I know the kid can't read. How about you?"

"Oh, sorry. I didn't notice." Tina pointed to the sign. "That says you can't eat in this cab. Wait till we get to the Port Authority."

The Port Authority was a big, big building with so many people. They got on a long line. Tina kept looking around as though she was scared. When they reached the counter, she asked about buses to Boston. The man said there was one at two-twenty they could make. Then a policeman started to walk toward them. Tina turned her face away and said under her breath, "Oh my God."

Jamie wondered if the policeman was going to make them go in a car the way they took Daddy. But he didn't come near them at all. Mommy used to tell her that policemen were her friends, but she knew that in New York it was different because Daddy and Tina were both afraid of them.

Tina brought her to where some people were sitting in a row of chairs. One old lady was asleep with her hand over her suitcase. Tina said, "Now, Jamie, you wait right here for me. I have to go on an errand and it may take a long time. Finish your hot dog and Coke and don't talk to anyone. If anyone talks to you, say you're with that lady."

Jamie was glad to sit down and have a chance to eat. The hot dog was cold and she wished it had mustard on it, but even so it tasted good. She watched Tina go back up the escalator.

She waited a long, long time. After a while, her eyes got heavy and she began to fall asleep. When she woke up, there were so many people hurrying past as though they were late for something. The old lady she was sitting next to was shaking her. "Are you alone?"

"No. Tina is coming right back." It was hard to talk. She was still so sleepy.

"All right, then. I have to catch my bus. Don't talk to anyone until Tina gets back."

Jamie had to go to the bathroom. Tina would be mad if she didn't wait for her, but she just couldn't not go to the bathroom. Then she heard the woman on the chair behind her say to her friend, "Let's go to the john before we leave."

She picked up the package with her new clothes and books and followed closely so it looked like she was with them.

In the bathroom there were so many

people and some of them had kids, so it was easy to go in and out of one of the stalls without anyone paying attention. She washed her hands and left the messy bathroom as fast as she could. For the first time she noticed the big clock on the wall. The little hand was on four. The big hand on one. That meant it was five after four. The man at the counter had told Tina the next bus was at two-twenty.

Jamie stopped, realizing Tina hadn't meant to take her on that bus at all. . . . Tina wasn't coming back.

Jamie knew that if she stayed here a policeman would start talking to her. She didn't knew where to go. Daddy wasn't home and Tina had gone away. She wanted so much to see Mommy. She knew she was going to start crying. It was Christmas Eve and she and Mommy were supposed to be together.

The big doors at the end of the room. People were going in and out of them. That must be the way out to the street. The package was heavy. She knew what she could do. The apartment was on Fifty-eighth Street and Seventh Avenue. If she could find the apartment, she could walk one block more to Central Park. From there she knew where the Plaza was. She would play the pretend game. She would pretend that Mommy was with her and they had had a carriage ride in Central Park and lunch at the Plaza. Then she'd go into the toy store across the street from the Plaza, just as she and Mommy had planned. She'd walk down Fifth Avenue and visit the baby Jesus and see the big tree and the Lord and Taylor windows.

She was out on the street. It was getting dark and the wind bit her cheeks. Her head felt cold without a hat. A man in a gray sweater and white apron was selling newspapers. She didn't want him to know she was alone so she pointed to a woman holding a baby and struggling to open a stroller. "We have to go to Fifty-eighth Street and Seventh Avenue," she told the man.

"You've got a long walk," he said. He waved his hand. "It's eighteen blocks up that way and one block over that way."

The plane was late departing and took an hour and forty minutes to LaGuardia Airport. It was three o'clock when she landed. She ran through the terminal.

As the cab snaked through the traffic on the Fifty-ninth Street Bridge, Susan tried not to remember that this was the day she and Jamie had planned to spend in New York.

At the police station, a Lieutenant Garrigan was waiting in his office.

"Have you found Jamie?"

"No, but I can assure you we're covering all the airports and bus stations." He showed her a mug shot. "Is this your former husband, Jeff Randall?"

"Is that what he's calling himself?"

"In New York, he's Jeff Randall. In Boston, Washington, Chicago and a dozen other cities he's someone else. It seems that he and his girlfriend have been posing as wealthy out-of-towners

MAP OF PLACES MENTIONED
IN THE SELECTION

New York City, NEW YORK

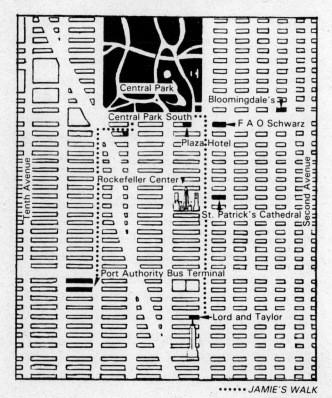

looking for a co-op in New York. Having the little girl with them has made the act more convincing."

"Can I speak to Jeff?" Susan asked.

He hadn't changed in the last year. The same wavy brown hair, the same guileless blue eyes, the same ready smile, the same concerned, protective manner. "Susan, it's good to see you. You're looking very well. Thinner, but it's becoming."

They might have been old friends bumping into each other unexpectedly. "Where would this woman take Jamie?" Susan asked. She clenched her hands, afraid she would hammer his face with her fists.

"What are you talking about?"

They were sitting across from each other in the small, crowded office. The lieutenant was still behind his desk. "You're liable to be spending enough years in prison without adding a kidnapping charge," he said. "I would imagine your former wife might drop that complaint if your little girl is found immediately."

He would not answer any questions, not even when Susan's control snapped and she screamed at him, "I'll kill you if anything happens to her." She bit her hand to hold back the racking sobs as they took Jeff away.

The lieutenant brought her to a waiting room. Someone brought her coffee. Susan tried to pray but could not find any words. Only one thought echoed in her mind, insistent. "I want Jamie. I want Jamie."

At ten after four, Lieutenant Garrigan told her that a clerk in the Port Authority remembered that a woman with a child resembling Jamie's description had bought tickets on the two-twenty bus to Boston. They were wiring ahead to have it checked at one of the rest stops. At four-thirty it was determined that they were not on the bus. At quarter of five Tina was picked up at Newark Airport as she tried to board a plane to Los Angeles.

Lieutenant Garrigan tried to sound optimistic as he told Susan what they had learned. "Tina left Jamie sitting in the waiting room of the Port Authority Terminal. One of the transit cops is still on duty. He remembers seeing a child answering her description leave with two women."

"They could have taken her anywhere," Susan whispered. "What kind of people wouldn't take a lost child to the police?"

"Some women will take a lost child home first and ask their husbands what to do," the lieutenant said. "Believe me, you're a lot better off if that's what's happened. It means she's safe. I wouldn't want to think Jamie is wandering around Manhattan alone today. There are an awful lot of weirdos on the streets during the holidays. They try to spot kids who have gotten separated from adults."

He must have seen the terror on Susan's face because he added quickly,

"We're going to try to get an appeal on the radio stations and have her picture on the evening news. That Tina woman says Jamie knows the address of the apartment and the telephone number. We've got an officer in the apartment in case anyone calls. Maybe you'd like to wait there. It's just a few blocks away. I'll send you in a squad car."

A young cop was watching television in the living room. Susan walked through the apartment, noticing a dish with a few dried cornflakes on the dinette table, the coloring books stacked beside it. The smaller bedroom . . . the bed was unmade, the imprint of a head on the pillow. Jamie had slept here last night.

Susan felt her lungs closing, her lips quivering, hysteria rising in her chest. She walked over to the window, opened it and drank in the fresh air. Glancing down she could see the traffic on Seventh Avenue. To the left, Central Park South was lined with horses and carriages. Her eyes blurred as she saw a family turn from Seventh Avenue onto Central Park South. The mother and father were ahead. Their three children trailing behind, the two boys shoving each other, a little girl close on their heels.

Christmas Eve. She and Jamie were supposed to be here together. They were going to have their special day. A sudden, irrational thought flashed through Susan's mind—Suppose Jamie wasn't with those women after all. . . . Suppose she was alone.

The policeman, his attention thoroughly diverted from the television, took down the places she named. "I'll call the lieutenant," he promised. "We'll comb Fifth Avenue for her."

Susan grabbed her coat. "So will I."

Jamie's feet were so tired. She had walked and walked and walked. At first she counted every block, but then she saw that the signs on the corners showed the numbers. Forty-three, forty-four.

She was very careful to walk near mothers and fathers and other kids. Mommy had told her about that. "If you're ever lost, always go to someone with children." But she didn't want to talk to any of these people. She wanted to play the pretend game.

She knew when she reached Fifty-eighth Street. She could tell by the stores. The apartment was on this block.

A man came up to her and took her hand. She tried to pull away but could not. "You're alone, aren't you, darling?" he whispered.

He wouldn't let go of her hand. He was smiling, but somehow he looked scary. It was hard to see his eyes because they were narrow. He was wearing a dirty jacket and his pants hung on him. She knew she shouldn't tell him she was alone.

"No," she said quickly. "Mommy and I are hungry." She pointed into the pizza shop and a lady who was buying pizza looked out and kind of smiled.

The man dropped her hand. "I thought you needed help."

Jamie waited till he walked across the street and then she began to run down the block. When she was three buildings away, she saw a police car pull up to the apartment house. For just a minute she was so scared that they had come to get her too. But then a woman got out and ran in the building and the car drove away. She rubbed the back of her hand across her eyes. It was so babyish to cry.

When she got to the apartment house, she kept her head down. She didn't want anyone to see her and maybe stop her and take her to jail too. But the box was so heavy. As she passed the building, she stopped and put the box behind the stone flower boxes. Maybe she could just leave it here for a while.

It was so much easier to walk without the box. She turned at the corner and looked back. The man in the dirty jacket was following her. That scared her a little. She was glad that some people

walked past her, a mother and a father
and two boys. She hurried to get close
to them. The group came to the corner
and turned right. She knew that was the
way she was supposed to go. Central
Park was across the street. Now she
could start to play the pretend game.

Susan hurried along Central Park
South, going from one to the other of the
drivers in the hansom cabs.

The drivers wanted to help. They all
studied the picture of Jamie in the magazine. "Pretty little girl . . . She looks like
an angel." They all promised to keep an
eye out for her.

Susan held the magazine open to
Jamie's picture. Over and over she
asked, "Have you seen her?"

No one at the Plaza remembered seeing
a child alone. F A O Schwarz was her next
stop. No one remembered seeing an
unaccompanied child. She went to the
second floor. A clerk studied the picture
thoughtfully. "I can't be sure. I'm much
too busy. But there was a little girl who

asked to hold a Minnie Mouse rag doll. Her father wanted to buy it for her, but she said no. I thought it was peculiar. Yes, indeed, there's a striking resemblance to this child."

"But she was with her father," Susan murmured, adding, "thank you."

The clerk stared after Susan as she got on the escalator. Come to think of it, what child who obviously wants a doll doesn't let her father buy it for her? And there'd been something creepy about that guy. Ignoring an insistent customer, the clerk ran from behind the counter to catch Susan. Too late—Susan had already disappeared.

Seeing the Minnie Mouse doll had made Jamie want to cry and cry. But she couldn't let that man buy her a present. She knew that. She was scared that he was still following her.

Outside the toy store the streets weren't quite as crowded now. She guessed everybody was going home. On one of the corners people were singing

Christmas carols. She stopped and listened to them. She knew the man who was following her had stopped too. The women singers had bonnets on instead of hats. One of them smiled at her when the song was finished. Jamie smiled back, and the woman said, "Little girl, you're not alone, are you?" Jamie said, "Mommy's with me. She's right over there." She pointed at the crowd of people looking in the windows of a store and hurried toward them.

In St. Patrick's Cathedral she stopped and gazed around. Finally she found the manger. There were a lot of people standing around it, but the baby Jesus wasn't in the crib. A man was putting new candles in holders and Jamie heard a lady ask where the statue of the Infant was. "It's placed during Midnight Mass," he told her.

Jamie managed to find a place right in front of the crib. She whispered the prayer she had been saying for so long.

"When you come tonight, bring Mommy too. Please."

There were so many people coming into the church. The organ began to play. She loved the sound of it. It would be good to sit here a while where it was nice and warm and rest. But somehow just telling the lady who was singing that Mommy was with her made it seem so real. She'd go to the tree now and then to the Lord and Taylor windows. After that if the man was still following her, maybe she would ask him what she should do. Maybe if he liked her enough to keep following her, he really did want to take care of her.

Susan's eyes scanned the faces of the children as she passed. One little girl made her catch her breath, the golden hair, a red jacket. But it wasn't Jamie. Every few blocks, there were volunteers dressed as Santa Claus collecting for charity. To each one of them, she showed Jamie's picture. A Salvation

Army choir was singing on the corner of Fifty-third Street. One of them had seen a little girl who certainly looked like Jamie. But the child had said she was with her mother.

Lieutenant Garrigan caught up with her just as she was about to go into the cathedral. He was in a squad car. Susan saw the pity in his eyes as he glanced at the picture she was holding.

"I'm afraid you're wasting your time, Susan," he said. "A Trailways bus driver said two women and a small girl were on his four-ten run out of the Port Authority. That jives with the time the transit cop saw them leave."

"I still think we have a chance of a phone call from those women . . . if they took her. CBS has agreed to let you make a special appeal just before the seven o'clock news. But we'll have to hurry."

"Could we drive down Fifth to Lord and Taylor's?" Susan asked. "I don't know—I just have this feeling . . ."

At her insistence the squad car drove

slowly. Susan's head turned from side to side as she tried to see the passersby on both sides of the street.

She insisted that they stop in front of Lord and Taylor's. People were patiently lining up to walk past the fairyland displays. "I just think that if Jamie were in New York and remembered . . ." She bit her lip. She knew that Lieutenant Garrigan thought she was being foolish.

The little girl in the blue and green snowsuit. About Jamie's size. No. The child half-hidden behind the stocky man. She studied her eagerly, then shook her head.

Lieutenant Garrigan touched her sleeve. "I honestly think the best thing you can do for Jamie is to broadcast the appeal on television."

Reluctantly Susan agreed.

Jamie watched the ice skaters. They were skimming around the rink in front of the Christmas tree.

Jamie turned away from the tree. She had just one more place to see, the Lord and Taylor's windows. The man and woman next to her were holding hands. She tugged at the woman's arm. "My mother asked me to ask you how far it is to Lord and Taylor's."

Twelve more blocks. That was a lot. But she had to finish the pretend game. It was starting to snow harder. She didn't look to see if the man was still following her—she knew he was. But as long as she walked next to other people he didn't come too close.

The squad car pulled up to the CBS studios at Fifty-seventh Street near Eleventh Avenue. Lieutenant Garrigan went inside with her. They were sent upstairs and a production assistant talked with Susan. "We're going to call this segment 'The Lost Angel.' We'll do a closeup of Jamie's picture, and then you can make a special appeal."

Susan waited in the corner of the television studio. Something seemed to be bursting inside her. It was as though she could hear Jamie's voice calling her. Lieutenant Garrigan was waiting with her. She grabbed his arm. "Tell them to show the picture. Let someone else make the appeal. I've got to go back."

Jamie waited on the line to walk in front of the windows at Lord and Taylor's. They were as beautiful as Mommy had promised, like paintings from her fairytale books except that the figures moved and bent and waved. She found herself waving back. They were pretend people. It was almost as though they understood the pretend game. "Next year," Jamie whispered, "Mommy and I will come back together." She wanted to stay here, to keep watching the beautiful figures bend and turn and smile, but someone kept saying, "Please keep moving. Thank you."

The trouble was the pretend game was over. She had been everywhere she and Mommy had planned to go. Now she didn't know what to do. Her forehead was wet with snow and she brushed her hair back.

She didn't want to stop looking in the

windows. She squeezed herself against the rope so that people could pass her. "You're lost, aren't you, dear?" She looked up. It was the man who had been following her. He was talking so low she could hardly hear him. "If you know where you live, I could take you home," he whispered.

A bubble of hope grew in Jamie's chest. "Would you please phone my mother?" she asked. "I know the number."

"Of course. Let's go right now." He reached for her hand.

"Please keep moving," the voice said again.

"Come on," the man whispered. "We have to go."

There was something hurting Jamie. It was more than being tired and cold and hungry. She was scared. She clung to the edge of the windows, stared at the doll figures and whispered her baby Jesus prayer. "Please, please let Mommy come now."

* * *

The squad car pulled up. "I know you think I'm crazy," Susan said. Her voice trailed off as she studied the still-dense crowd around the windows. There were a number of children in the line, but it was impossible to see their faces because they were facing the store windows. She was opening the door when she heard Lieutenant Garrigan say to the driver, "Sam, do you see who's on that line? It's that stinking child molester who didn't show up for trial. Come on!"

Shocked, Susan watched as they dashed across the sidewalk, pushed through the line, grabbed the arms of the skinny man in a dirty jacket and hurried him back toward the squad car.

And then she saw her. The small figure who did not turn around with the rest of the astonished bystanders, the small figure with the cap of unfamiliar white-gold hair that curved around the familiar cheek and neck.

Dazedly, Susan walked toward Jamie. Her hungry arms stretched out, she bent over and listened as Jamie continued to beg, "Please, please let Mommy come now."

Susan sank to her knees. "Jamie," she whispered. Jamie thought she was still playing the pretend game.

"Jamie."

It wasn't pretend. Jamie spun around and felt arms close around her. *Mommy.* It was *Mommy.* She locked her arms around Mommy's neck. She dug her head into Mommy's shoulder. Mommy was hugging her so tight. Mommy was rocking her. Mommy was saying her name over and over. "Jamie, Jamie." Mommy was crying. And in the fairyland windows, the beautiful dolls were bowing and waving.

Jamie patted Mommy's cheek. "I knew you'd come," she whispered.

ITEM CHARGED

LIB#: *1000211258*
GRP: STUDENT

Due: 5/7/2013 08:00 PM

Title: Selected from The lost angel / Mary
Higgins Clark.
Auth: Clark, Mary Higgins.
Call #: 428.64 CLARK 1990
Enum
Chron
Copy:
Item *00210137*

ABOUT
MARY HIGGINS CLARK

Mary Higgins was born on December 24, 1931. She grew up in New York City. After high school, Mary worked as a secretary. She wanted to see the world, so she became an airline stewardess.

After a year as a stewardess, she married Warren Clark. They had five children. While raising her family, Mary Higgins Clark began to write. It took her six years to get her first story published.

When her husband suddenly died of a heart attack, she turned to writing to help support the family. She got up at 5 A.M. and wrote until 7 A.M. Then she went to a 9-to-5 job. She published her first novel when she was 47 years old.

Mary Higgins Clark's hard work paid off, for today she is one of the most successful fiction writers in the United States. She often speaks and writes to support literacy. She says, "Reading is the key to education, to getting ahead, to having a bigger life."

ABOUT PARENTAL KIDNAPPING

In *The Lost Angel,* Jamie's father is a jewel thief. He kidnaps Jamie so she can go with him when he cases apartments to rob. Most reasons why parents kidnap their children are not as dramatic as this.

Many divorced or separated parents who kidnap their children do so because of bad feelings between them. Sometimes parents think that they don't have a fair child custody agreement, and they feel that kidnapping is the only way they will be able to see their children.

Sometimes one parent thinks that the other is harming the child. Or the parents may disagree about the right way to raise or educate the child.

No matter what the reasons, kidnapping can be devastating for the child. The child usually misses the other parent very much and is confused about what is happening.

Nearly every state has criminal laws to prevent and punish parental kidnapping, but the laws differ from state to state. In addition, national laws have been passed to prevent kidnapping.

A good place to get information or help is the National Center for Missing and Exploited Children (NCMEC). The NCMEC runs a toll-free hotline (1–800–843–5678). Parents can call this number to report a missing child. So can people with information about a missing child.

The NCMEC publishes a free 75-page booklet called *Parental Kidnapping: How to Prevent an Abduction and What to Do If Your Child Is Abducted.* You can get a copy by calling the hotline listed above.

The NCMEC also offers many other booklets free of charge that deal with the safety of children. You can write to the address below and ask for more information:


```
National Center for Missing
    and Exploited Children
2101 Wilson Blvd., Suite 550
     Arlington, VA 22201
```

QUESTIONS FOR THE READER

Thinking about the Story

1. What did you think about the selection from *The Lost Angel*? What did you like or not like?

2. Are there ways that the events or people became important or special to you? Write about or discuss these.

3. In what ways did the selection answer the questions you had before you began reading or listening?

4. Were any parts of the selection difficult to understand? If so, you may want to read or listen to them again. You might think about why they were difficult.

Thinking about the Writing

1. How did Mary Higgins Clark help you see, hear, and feel what happened in the selection? Find the words, phrases, or sentences that did this best.

2. Writers think carefully about their stories' settings, characters, and events. In writing this selection, which of these things do you think Mary Higgins Clark

felt was most important? Find the parts of the story that support your opinion.

3. In the selection, Mary Higgins Clark uses dialogue. Dialogue can make a story stronger and more alive. Pick out some dialogue that you feel is strong, and explain how it helps the story.

4. *The Lost Angel* is written from the point of view of someone outside the story who tells us what is happening. The writer uses the words "he" and "she." Yet the parts of the story that tell about what Susan does are different from the parts that tell about Jamie. How does Mary Higgins Clark create a child's world in the parts about Jamie?

Activities

1. Were there any words that were difficult for you in the selection from *The Lost Angel*? Go back to these words and try to figure out their meanings. Discuss what you think each word means, and why you made that guess. Discuss with your teacher or another student how you are going to remember each word. Some

ways to remember words are to put them on file cards, or write them in your journal, or create a personal dictionary. Be sure to use the words in your writing in a way that will help you to remember their meaning.

2. How did you help yourself understand the selections? Did you ask yourself questions? What were they? Discuss these questions with other people who have read the same selection, or write them in your journal.

3. Talking with other people about what you have read can increase your understanding of it. Discussion can help you organize your thoughts, get new ideas, and rethink your original ideas. Discuss your thoughts about the selection with someone else who has read it. Find out if your opinions are the same or different. See if your thoughts change as a result of this discussion.

4. After you finish reading or listening, you might want to write down your thoughts about the book. You could

write a book review, or a letter to a friend you think might be interested in the book. You could write your reflections in your journal, or you could write about topics the book has brought up.

5. Did reading the selection give you any ideas for your own writing? You might want to write about:

• a time when you or someone you know was lost.

• the love of parents and children for each other.

• a holiday season when you had problems to cope with.

6. You might want to help parents in your community whose children have run away or are missing. You could make up a list of the agencies in your area that help find children. You could help make a poster of a missing child.

7. If you could talk to Mary Higgins Clark, what questions would you ask about her writing? You might want to write the questions in your journal.